Hercules the Hero

WHITE WOLVES

Hercules the Hero

Tony Bradman
Illustrated by Steve May

A & C Black • London

White Wolves Series Consultant: Sue Ellis,
Centre for Literacy in Primary Education

This book can be used in the White Wolves Guided Reading programme
with Year 3 children who have an average level of reading experience

First published 2008 by
A & C Black Publishers Ltd
38 Soho Square, London, W1D 3HB

www.acblack.com

Text copyright © 2008 Tony Bradman
Illustrations copyright © 2008 Steve May

The rights of Tony Bradman and Steve May to be identified
as author and illustrator of this work respectively have been
asserted by them in accordance with the Copyrights,
Designs and Patents Act 1988.

ISBN 978-0-7136-8717-0

A CIP catalogue for this book is available from the British Library.

This book is produced using paper that is made from wood grown
in managed, sustainable forests. It is natural, renewable and
recyclable. The logging and manufacturing processes conform
to the environmental regulations of the country of origin.

Printed and bound in Great Britain
by CPI Cox & Wyman, Reading RG1 8EX.

Contents

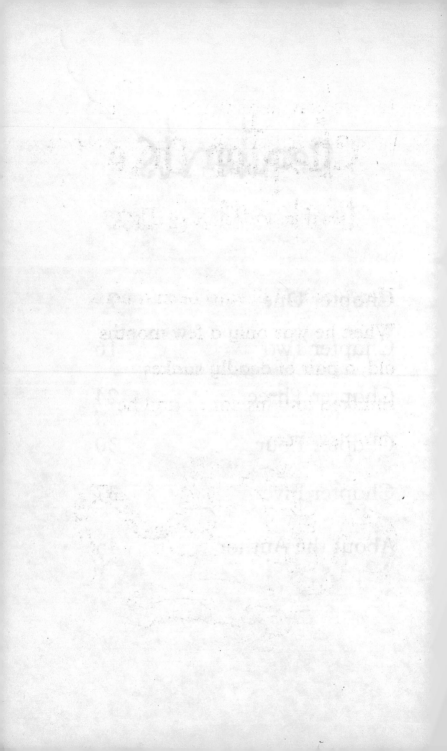

chapter one
trouble with a goddess

Hercules had always been a hero.
When he was only a few months
old, a pair of deadly snakes
slithered into his cot ... and he
throttled them.

As he was growing up, Hercules
did many amazing things.

By the time he
was a young man,
he was famous in
Greece for his
strength and
courage.

There was
nothing he liked
better than a
challenge, and
he had a sense
of humour, too.
Everybody liked him, and thought
he was terrific.

Everybody, that is, except one of the Immortal Gods. High up in her home on lofty Mount Olympus, the Goddess Hera was scowling. She didn't like to see a mere *human* having all that fame and success...

"Look at Hercules strutting around," she said. "It makes me so cross."

"Steady on, old girl," said her husband, the great God Zeus, raising a colossal eyebrow. "That's a bit unfair. He's just a lad out to have fun."

"Oh, is he now?" said Hera, glaring. "Well, I could do with some fun myself. It's been really boring up here recently. See you later, Zeus!"

At that moment, Hercules was strolling towards Thebes, his home town. Suddenly, the air shimmered strangely, and Hera appeared! He recognised the goddess from the statues in her temples, and fell to his knees.

"Hail, mighty Hera!" he said, because he knew he should be polite to any Immortals he might meet. "Most wondrous goddess..."

"Spare me the flattery,"
snapped Hera. "I know you
don't mean it."

"But ... I do!" said Hercules.
"Honestly, I think you're..."

"I don't *care* what you think,"
said Hera. "I'm not very happy
with *you*, Hercules. It's time you
were taught a lesson."

Hercules opened his mouth to speak, but it was too late. There was more shimmering, and then he felt himself flying through the air. He landed with a *thump*! on a marble floor and sprang to his feet, ready for anything.

He looked around and realised
he was in the hall of somebody's
palace. A nasty-looking man was
sitting on a large throne, staring
at him.

"Meet your new master,
Hercules," said Hera. "You are
now the slave of King Eurystheus."

Hercules frowned. Eurystheus was King of Tiryns. He was a cruel man, who loved making people suffer.

"But mighty Hera, I don't understand..." said Hercules. "Why are you doing this to me? What lesson do you think I need to be taught?"

"Silence, mortal!" snapped Hera. "How dare you question me!" She was going to enjoy seeing Hercules put in his place at last...

Chapter Two

Some interesting little jobs

Hercules was still feeling confused. But then he sighed. Hera was an Immortal Goddess, so it was his duty to obey her.

"I hear you're supposed to be a hero," said Eurystheus with a sneer. "Well, I've got a few ... *interesting* little jobs for you."

"No problem," said Hercules. "What would you like me to do?"

"Go to Nemea," said
Eurystheus, with an evil smile.
"A wild beast is causing trouble
on my farms there."

A few days later, Hercules
arrived in the valley of Nemea.
It was full of olive groves and
fields and farms, but everywhere
was strangely quiet.

Suddenly, Hercules heard a low growling. He turned round, and there was an *enormous* lion staring at him with its yellow eyes.

"So *this* is what he calls an interesting little job," Hercules murmured.

The lion *roared*! and leapt at him, but Hercules dived out of the way. He scrambled to his feet, broke a thick branch off the nearest olive tree ... and bashed the lion over the head.

Hercules returned to the palace, wearing the lion's skin and carrying a big, olive-wood club.

Eurystheus was having his lunch, and nearly choked on it. Hera was surprised, too.

"Anything else I can do for you, master?" Hercules said cheerfully.

"Er ... hang on a second," said Eurystheus, thinking hard.

Then he smiled. "I want you to kill the Hydra. That won't be quite so easy..."

"Good suggestion," whispered Hera. "You're supposed to be giving him a hard time."

"Oh, don't worry," said Eurystheus. "I promise you I'll make his life a misery."

Hercules set off to do the job. He knew all about the Hydra. It was a giant serpent with nine heads full of fangs. It was said that if you cut off any of the heads, another two would instantly grow in its place.

"How am I going to deal with you?" said Hercules when he was facing the hideous creature. "Nine heads, and all of them ugly."

The Hydra hissed and snapped at him.

"I know! I need some fire and steel..." Hercules lit a flaming torch and whipped out his sword. Every time he hacked off a head, he burned the stump before a new head could grow. Soon the beast was totally headless ... and dead.

This time, Eurystheus nearly choked on his supper when Hercules returned. The people of Tiryns had heard what he'd done,

and the road
to the palace
was lined
with cheering
crowds.

Hera was
not so pleased.

"What are
you playing at,
Eurystheus?" she said.
"I thought you were
going to make his life
a misery. But that's
not happening, is it?"

"Just you wait," said the king.
"He hasn't seen anything yet..."

Chapter Three

a busy few weeks

Hercules soon had another task
to face, and another, and another.
In fact, it was a busy few weeks for
him. Eurystheus made sure each
"little job" was harder than the last,
and they were all very different.

He told Hercules to bring him
the Deer With The Golden Horns,
a creature that could run as fast
as the wind. Luckily, Hercules
could run faster.

Then there was the Brutal
Boar, a huge, terrifying beast that
had killed hundreds of hunters.

Hercules
quickly
had him
trussed
up,
though.

Next
was a big
cleaning
job. A
certain
King Augeas kept a herd of cattle
in his stables, and the place had
never been cleaned.

So the poor cattle were knee deep in their own dung. Augeas said Hercules had to clean the stables – *in just one day*.

Hercules started by shovelling out the dung. But he soon realised he would never get rid of it in the time he had.

He stood scratching his head.
Then he had a brilliant idea.
He simply diverted the local river
through the stables ... and left
them smelling sweet.

"A neat trick, though I say
so myself!" said Hercules, and
laughed.

"If there's one thing I hate it's a clever-clogs," muttered Eurystheus when Hercules returned. "But you haven't got the better of me yet!"

The tasks came thick and fast after that. Hercules shot down the Bronze Birds of Stymphalos, whose beaks were deadly. He wrestled with the Great Bull of Crete and captured it, wrecking most of Crete in the process.

He rounded up the Man-eating
Horses of King Diomedes.

When he got back to Tiryns,
the people were most impressed.

"I don't believe it," muttered
Eurystheus. "Right, I want you
to get me the belt of the Amazon
queen. Those girls will tear you
to pieces…"

Chapter Four

a battle ... and some apples

Hercules had heard of the
Amazons. They were incredibly
fierce women warriors, and their
queen was the
toughest of them
all. He asked
her nicely if
he could have
her belt, but
she yelled:
"Get him, girls!"

There was a terrific battle
that lasted for hours, and Hercules
just managed to hold them off.
Finally, he grabbed the belt ...
and ran.

"Sorry!" he called out, as
the Amazons chased after him.
"But I need it!"

Next Eurystheus made him
steal the White Cattle of Geryon,
an ogre with six arms and three
heads. Hercules used his club on
Geryon's heads as if he were
playing the drums, knocking him
out so he could
take the cattle.

Then he was sent to fetch the
Golden Apples of Paradise...

The problem was that only the giant Atlas knew where they were, and he was busy holding up the sky. So Hercules offered to take the sky from him while Atlas fetched the apples.

Atlas did as he was asked ... but then decided he was enjoying life without his great burden, and refused to shoulder it again.

"Fair enough," said Hercules. "I'm happy to do the job. But could you take it back for just one second? I've got a crick in my neck..."

Atlas shrugged, took the sky again ... and Hercules escaped.

Eurystheus and Hera were waiting at the palace, as usual. They both scowled when Hercules tipped the golden apples onto the floor.

They could hear a huge crowd outside chanting their hero's name – "Hercules! *Hercules*! HERCULES!"

"This is *not* going well, Eurystheus," Hera hissed. "He's done everything you told him to, and now he's more famous than ever!"

"OK, we need something that's impossible," said the king, looking worried. "I've got it! I'll make him bring me the Hound of Hades…"

chapter Five
to hell and back

"So you want me to bring you Cerberus, the giant, three-headed dog that guards the entrance to Hades," sighed Hercules. "Is that all?"

"Off you go," said Eurystheus. "And stop looking so smug. Even *you* won't be able to do this."

"You'd better hope so, Eurystheus," muttered Hera. "I'm nearly out of patience."

It took Hercules a while to make his way down to Hades, which was the Greeks' name for Hell. He went into a cave, then followed a long, dark tunnel down to the River Styx. He had to pay Charon the ferryman to take him across the thick, black water in a creaky old boat. Ghosts flittered and twittered around their heads.

At last, Hercules stood at the gateway to Hades. And there was Cerberus, a huge beast, its three heads all barking at once, drool dripping from its pointed fangs, its six eyes burning red as they stared at him.

Hercules gulped. He knew it would be incredibly hard to capture such a creature. Then he had another brilliant idea...

Hercules had never met a dog who didn't enjoy running around in the fresh air. And poor Cerberus spent all his time down here in the dark.

"Hey, Cerberus," Hercules said. "Would you like to go ... walkies?"

Cerberus stopped barking *instantly*, and all six ears pricked up...

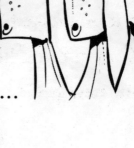

Eurystheus nearly choked on his dinner when Hercules returned this time – with the Hound of Hades on a leash. The king was so scared he climbed into a big jar to hide.

Hercules picked it up and emptied him out. "I've done what you asked," he said. "Wouldn't you like to play with your new pet?"

He let Cerberus off the leash,
and the dog barked with joy ...
and chased the screaming king
round and round the hall.

Suddenly, Hera shimmered into view, and Hercules fell to his knees. "Forgive me, mighty Hera, I beg you," he said. "I just couldn't bear to be at that man's beck and call any more. I'll call off the dog…"

"Don't you dare, Hercules," said Hera, laughing. "That's the funniest thing I've seen in ages. Maybe you're not such a bad lad after all!"

Hercules laughed, too. From that day on they were the best of friends, and Hercules went on to have many more exciting adventures. As for Eurystheus ... well, some people say he's still running from Cerberus.

But the Immortal Gods couldn't possibly be that cruel, could they?

About the Author

Tony Bradman was born in London and still lives there. He has written a large number of books for children of all ages and edited many anthologies of poetry and short stories.

Tony has always loved reading great stories from the past, and has written retellings of many of the great myths. He says that everyone should know something about Hercules, one of the greatest heroes of all time!

Other White Wolves Myths and Legends...

ARTHUR'S SWORD

Sophie McKenzie

Arthur is a better sword fighter than his
foster brother, Kay, but *he's* not the one
training to be a knight. So he's thrilled to
meet Merlin, who promises to help him
become Kay's squire. Then the king dies,
and Arthur gets the chance to carry out his
first big challenge. There's a sword stuck in
a rock, and no one can pull it free...

Arthur's Sword is a modern retelling
of the classic legend of old.

ISBN: 9 780 7136 8815 3 £4.99

Other White Wolves Myths and Legends...

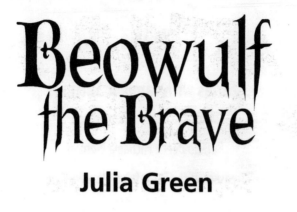

Beowulf the Brave

Julia Green

The king of Denmark is in trouble. His people are living in terror of a monster that no one can kill. So the brave warrior Beowulf takes up the challenge. He sets sail with fourteen men, and arrives at the king's hall. That night, he slays the monster in a bloody battle, but now his problems have just begun…

Beowulf the Brave is a modern retelling of the classic Anglo-Saxon legend.

ISBN: 9 780 7136 8841 2 £4.99

Year 3

Stories with Familiar Settings

Detective Dan • Vivian French

Buffalo Bert • Michaela Morgan

Treasure at the Boot-fair • Chris Powling

Mystery and Adventure Stories

Scratch and Sniff • Margaret Ryan

The Thing in the Basement • Michaela Morgan

On the Ghost Trail • Chris Powling

Myths and Legends

Pandora's Box • Rose Impey

Sephy's Story • Julia Green

Wings of Icarus • Jenny Oldfield

Arthur's Sword • Sophie McKenzie

Hercules the Hero • Tony Bradman

Beowulf the Brave • Julia Green